It's Super to Be to Be Six!

NO AR

It's Super to Be Six!

A
LITTLE APPLE
PAPERBACK

SCHOLASTIC INC.

New York   Toronto   London   Auckland   Sydney
Mexico City   New Delhi   Hong Kong

Table of Contents

Introduction

Now that you are six, you can do lots of fun things. You can go to school. You can play detective. You can learn how to ride a bike.

In this book, you will meet lots of six-year-olds just like you. There are Sparky and Eddie, who are starting the first grade. There is Nate, who is helping Rosamond to find her lost cat. There are Molly and Mary Beth, who are learning to bake cookies for their Pee Wee Scouts project.

This book will make you laugh and cheer for all the fun things six-year-olds can do. And now that you are six, you can read these stories all by yourself!

The End

When I was One,
I had just begun.

When I was Two,
I was nearly new.

When I was Three,
I was hardly me.

When I was Four,
I was not much more.

When I was Five,
I was just alive.

But now I am Six, I'm as clever as clever.
So I think I'll be six now for ever and ever.

From

Danny and the Dinosaur

by Syd Hoff

Danny loves dinosaurs. In fact, he wishes he had one. Then one day his wish comes true!

One day Danny went
to the museum.
He wanted to see what was inside.

He saw Indians.

He saw bears.

He saw Eskimos.

He saw guns.

He saw swords.

And he saw…

DINOSAURS!

Danny loved dinosaurs.

He wished he had one.

"I'm sorry they are not real,"
said Danny.

"It would be nice to play
with a dinosaur."

"And I think it would be nice
to play with you," said a voice.

"Can you?" said Danny.

"Yes," said the dinosaur.

"Oh, good," said Danny.

"What can we do?"

"I can take you for a ride,"
said the dinosaur.

He put his head down
so Danny could get on him.

"Let's go!" said Danny.

A policeman stared at them.

He had never seen a dinosaur
stop for a red light.

The dinosaur was so tall Danny had
to hold up the ropes for him.

"Look out!" said Danny.

"Bow wow!" said a dog.

"He thinks you are a car,"

said Danny. "Go away, dog.
We are not a car."
"I can make a noise like a car,"
said the dinosaur.
"Honk! Honk! Honk!"
"What big rocks," said the dinosaur.
"They are not rocks," said Danny.
"They are buildings."
"I love to climb," said the dinosaur.
"Down, boy!" said Danny.
The dinosaur had to be very careful
not to knock over houses or stores
with his long tail.
Some people were waiting for a bus.
They rode on the dinosaur's tail
instead.

"All who want to cross the street
may walk on my back,"
said the dinosaur.

"It's very nice of you
to help me with my
bundles," said a lady.
Danny and the dinosaur went
all over town and had lots of fun.

"It's good to take an hour or two off after a hundred million years," said the dinosaur.

From NATE THE GREAT

by Marjorie Weinman Sharmat

Nate is a detective. He likes to eat pancakes. And he likes to solve cases. He has found a pair of lost slippers, balloons, and even a goldfish. Today he is working on a big case for his friend Annie. But first he must help Rosamond find her missing cat.

I, Nate the Great, had something to say.

"I am hungry."

"Would you like some more
pancakes?" Annie asked.

I could tell that Annie was
a smart girl.

I hate to eat on the job.

But I must keep up my strength.

We sat in the kitchen.

Cold pancakes are almost
as good as hot pancakes.

"Now, on with the case," I said.

"Next we will talk
to your friend Rosamond."

Annie and I walked
to Rosamond's house.

Rosamond had black hair

and green eyes.

And cat hair all over her.

"I am Nate the Great," I said.

"I am a detective."

"A detective?" said Rosamond.

"A real, live detective?"

"Touch me," I said.

"Prove you are a detective,"

said Rosamond.

"Find something. Find my lost cat."

"I am on a case," I said.

"I am on a big case."

"My lost cat is big," Rosamond said.

"His name is Super Hex.

I have four cats.

They are all named Hex."

I could tell that Rosamond
was a strange girl.
"Here are my other cats," she said.
"Big Hex, Little Hex, and
Plain Hex."
The cats had black hair
and green eyes.
And long claws.
Very long claws.
We went into Rosamond's house.
I looked around.
There were pictures everywhere.
Pictures of cats.
Sitting cats. Standing cats.
Cats in color and in black and white.
We sat down.

Little Hex jumped onto Annie's lap.

Plain Hex jumped onto
Rosamond's lap.

Big Hex jumped onto my lap.

I did not like Big Hex.

Big Hex did not like me.

"Time to go," I said.

"We just got here," Annie said.

She liked Little Hex.

"Time to go," I said again.

I stood up.

I tripped over something.

It was long and black.

It was a cat's tail.

"MEOW!"

"Super Hex!" Rosamond cried.

"You found him!
You are a detective."
"Of course," I said.
"He was under my chair.
Except for his tail."

Annie and I left.
It was a hard thing to do.
I could smell pancakes
in Rosamond's kitchen.

From SPARKY AND EDDIE:
THE FIRST DAY OF SCHOOL

by Tony Johnston

Sparky and Eddie are best friends. They love to climb trees. They love to look at bugs. They are always together. Now it is time for school. But Sparky and Eddie are not in the same classroom. What will they do?

Sparky and Eddie wanted

to start school.
They wanted to be
in the same room, too.
Their parents took them
to school one day to see who
their teachers would be.
The room lists were up.
Sparky would have Mr. Lopez.
Eddie would have Ms. Bean.
Sparky and Eddie looked
at each other.
They gasped,
"We're not in the same room!"
They felt glum.
Too glum to climb trees.
Too glum to look at bugs.

Too glum to even cry.
They stared at nothing, feeling glum.

Then Sparky said,
"Let's make a deal."
"What deal?" asked Eddie.

"We're not in the same room,"
said Sparky. "So we won't go to
school."

"COOL!" shouted Eddie.

"This year we'll stay home!"

"We'll climb trees," Sparky said.

"We'll look at bugs," Eddie said.

"We'll have fun, fun, FUN!"
shouted Sparky.

Then he said, "Shake on it."

So they did.

"No switchies?" asked Eddie.

"No switchies," Sparky said.

Eddie told his mother,

"Sparky and I made a deal.
We're not in the same room,

so we won't go to school this year."

"Oh, dear," said his mother.

"Your teacher will be sad."

Sparky told his father,

"Eddie and I made a deal.

We're not in the same room,

so we won't go to school this year."

"Oh, dear," said his father.

"Your teacher will be sad."

Eddie told Sparky,

"If we don't go to school,

our teachers will be sad."

"They'll whimper," said Sparky.

"They'll whine," Eddie said.

"They'll blubber."

"They'll cry like rain."

Sparky and Eddie felt so sad about
that, they almost cried like rain.
"What can we do?" Sparky asked.
Eddie thought.
He thought.
And thought.
Then Eddie said,
"We'll give them a chance.
If we like them, we'll stay."
"If we don't, we'll go home,"
said Sparky.
"We'll climb trees.
We'll look at bugs.
We'll have fun, fun, FUN!"
"This is a switchy," said Eddie.
"That's O.K.," said Sparky.

"It's a nice switchy. Is it a deal?"

"Deal," Eddie said.

And they shook on it.

TRAINING WHEELS

by Kathryn Cristaldi

*Alvin is learning how to ride a bike — without
training wheels. It is not easy. It is scary. What
happens if Alvin crashes?*

On Monday, Alvin said,
"Today is the day.
No more training wheels."

Alvin's little brother, Spike,
clapped his hands.

"Gurgle, gurgle," he said.

Alvin climbed onto his bike.

His dad took off the training wheels.

"Ready to roll," said Alvin's dad.

He held onto the back of the bike.

Alvin pushed off with his left foot.

Then his right.

Alvin's dad ran alongside the bike.

Then he said, "When you are going
fast enough, I will let go."

Alvin started to sweat.

He imagined himself crashing.

He imagined himself in the hospital
wrapped up like a mummy.

He could not speak.

He had to eat through a straw.

Alvin stopped pedaling.

"What is wrong?"

asked Alvin's dad.

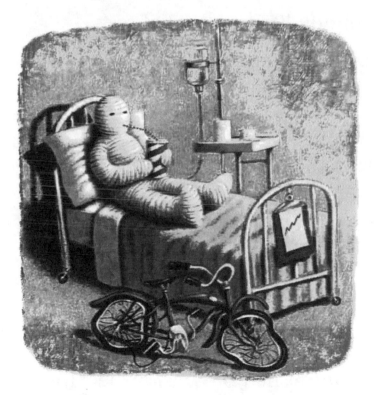

"My knees are weak," said Alvin.
"I think I am coming down
with the weak-knee flu."
"Okay," said Alvin's dad.
"But remember, son,
nobody likes a quitter."
On Tuesday, Alvin said,
"Today is the day.
No more training wheels."
Alvin's little brother, Spike,
clapped his hands.
"Gurgle, gurgle," he said.
Alvin climbed onto his bike.
His dad held onto the back.
"Ready to roll," said Alvin's dad.
Alvin pushed off with his left foot.

Then his right.

"This time I will not tell you
when I will let go," said Alvin's dad.

Alvin started to sweat.

He imagined himself flying
over the handlebars.

He imagined himself stuck in a tree.

Even the fire department
could not get him down.

Alvin stopped pedaling.

"What is wrong?" asked Alvin's dad.

"I just saw a UFO," said Alvin.

"It is headed for our house."

"Okay," said Alvin's dad.

"But remember, son,
nobody likes a quitter."

On Wednesday, Alvin's mom said,
"Alvin, can you watch Spike
for a minute?"
"Okay," said Alvin.
He was outside shining his bike.
It was a tough job.
He did not see Spike crawl
down the driveway.
He did not see Spike head
for the street.
Just then Alvin looked up.
A truck was coming
down the block.
Spike was in trouble!
Alvin jumped onto his bike.
He forgot all about

the training wheels.

He raced down the street

and grabbed Spike.

Safe!

At dinner, Alvin said, "I did it! I rode

my bike without training wheels!"

"Great!" said Alvin's parents.

"And I saved Spike from getting

crushed by a Mack truck!"

Alvin added.

Alvin's mom frowned.

"Remember, son," said Alvin's dad.

"Nobody likes a liar."

From PEE WEE SCOUTS:
COOKIES AND CRUTCHES

by Judy Delton

Molly and Mary Beth love being Pee Wee Scouts. They sing songs. They play games. And sometimes they make stuff. One day the scouts make cookies. Molly and Mary Beth work together. But baking cookies can turn into a yucky mess if you don't follow the recipe....

"We need something brown,"

said Mary Beth, opening
the refrigerator.

She reached for a bottle of root beer.

It was brown.

"Let's put some of this in," she said.

Molly looked doubtful.

It was brown, though.

And the cookie dough did look
too white.

She poured some of the root beer
into the batter.

Fizzzzz!

Little bubbles were all over.

Molly stirred it.

"It's too runny now," she said.

"We need something

to make it thick."

Mary Beth looked in the cupboard.
She reached for a package of
something that had a brown picture
on the box.

"What does this say?" she asked.

"Gravy mix," read Molly. "That's
good! My mom uses it to make
gravy thick when it's too runny.
So it would make this thick too."

Mary Beth dumped the box of
gravy mix into the cookie dough.

"Perfect!" said Molly.

"It's real thick now."

"Thick and brown!" said Mary Beth.

"It looks like Mrs. Peters's cookies."

"Now there is more dough,"
said Molly.

"But not enough chocolate chips!"
added Mary Beth.

"I like lots of chocolate chips,"
said Molly.

"So do I," said Mary Beth.

"That's the best part."

The girls looked in the cupboards
and in the refrigerator.

There were no more chips.

"We need something!" said
Mary Beth, stamping her foot.

"These look like chips," said Molly,
picking up a plastic bag.

"Dump them in!" said Mary Beth.

The girls stirred and stirred.
Then they put the cookies
on the pan one at a time,
as Mrs. Peters had shown them.
"Terrific!" said Molly.
"They look yummy!"
Mary Beth popped the pan
into the oven.
She set the timer for twelve minutes.
"Now all we do is wait," she said.
"Wait for our yummy
yummy cookies."
"Wash the dishes when you're
through," called Mary Beth's mother
from upstairs.
The girls sighed. Cookies were more

work than Mrs. Peters had said.
They washed the dishes and then
went to Mary Beth's room to wait.
Pretty soon Mary Beth's mother
called out, "What is that smell?"
The girls sniffed the air.
"It smells like turkey roasting,"
said Mrs. Kelly.
"Our cookies!" Molly shouted.

The cookies were not white now.
They were very very brown.
And they were huge.
"They look like hamburgers!"
said Molly.
"But they smell like turkey!"
said Mary Beth.

MY MAKE-BELIEVE DOG

by Gail Herman

Do you have any pets? The girl in this story thinks pets are the best. She asks her parents for a dog. But they say no. So the girl comes up with a plan. A plan to make them see pets are the best....

*I*n my first grade class, everybody has somebody.

Janie has a baby sister.

Beth has two brothers.

Annie has a dog.

I have no one.

"You are all so lucky!"

I tell my friends.

"Having a baby sister is lucky?"

says Janie. "Ha!"

"I am lucky to have two brothers?"

says Beth. "Ha, ha, ha!"

"You are right!" says Annie.

"My dog, Scamp, is the best!"

That is it! I say to myself.

Pets are the best!

"Hey, Mom,"

I say after school.

"Can we get a dog?"

"No," she says.

"Dogs make Dad sneeze."

"Hey, Dad," I say next.

"Can we get a dog?"

"No," he says.

"Dogs make Mom itch."

Sneeze? Itch? Ha!

They do not want a dog.

And that is all.

Maybe they do not know —

a dog would be fun!

All at once,

I have an idea.

A plan.

I will show them.

The next morning
I go to the backyard with Mom.
I throw a ball.
"What are you doing?"asks Mom.
"I am playing ball
with my new dog, Spot," I say.
"Isn't this fun?"
Mom goes in to speak to Dad.
I wait, then I listen
through the window.
"A make-believe dog!" Mom says.
"No walking. No feeding.
No trouble."
Uh-oh.
My plan is not working.
Mom and Dad think

a *real* dog will be trouble.

But I would take care of a dog.

Time for Plan B.

When Dad asks me

to help wash the car,

I say, "I can't.

I have to wash Spot."

When Mom asks me

to set the table,

I say, "Sorry, I have to walk Spot."

I am being a good owner!

But Mom and Dad are not happy.

Plan B is not working, either.

Good thing I have Plan C.

A real, live dog.

Annie brings Scamp right over.

"Isn't he cute?" I ask.

"Achoo!" says Dad.

Mom does not answer.

She is too busy scratching.

"Good-bye, Annie," I say.

"Good-bye, Scamp."

"We are sorry," says Mom.

"But we cannot have a dog."

Hmmm, I remember:

Pets are the best.

Time for Plan D!

The next morning, I ask Mom

for a glass of milk.

I pour the milk into a bowl.

"What are you doing?" Mom asks.

"I am feeding my new kitty-cat,"

I say. "Fluffy loves milk!"

From

LIAR, LIAR, PANTS ON FIRE!

by Miriam Cohen

Alex is the new kid in first grade. He wants to make friends. He tells everyone he has a pony. He says he has a rocket car that goes two thousand miles an hour. But the other kids know Alex is lying. Now no one wants to be friends with Alex. Until the day of the class Christmas party...

*F*irst grade was going to have a tree

that they decorated themselves.
Their teacher told them they were
supposed to use only things
that would be thrown away
such as plastic bottles, egg cartons,
cotton, and paper towel tubes.
Jim worked very hard on a
bleach–bottle Santa Claus.
His mother gave him a red sock
for a cap because the other sock
had been lost in the laundry.
He used cotton for a beard.
And he drew the nicest, kindest face.
When he put the crayon down,
he couldn't believe he had made
such a good Santa.

The morning of the Christmas party,
everybody hurried to school,
carrying their decorations.
Louie's was a folded paper bird with
wings that could move. Margaret had
a picture of her baby brother pasted
in a little cardboard box-bed.
It had a tiny cotton blanket.
Willy and Sammy made a train
with Santa riding in one of the cars.
"He's taking the uptown express
to our houses," they said.
Jim's Santa's cap was lost.
When he went to look for it,
Alex had found it.
"Here," he said. "It was outside."

"Oh boy, thanks!" said Jim.
Everybody was laughing
and running around.
The teacher said, "Line up, please!
We'll take turns putting our
decorations on the tree. Alex,
didn't you make anything?"
Alex looked at the floor.
"I didn't know how," he said.
Suddenly Jim felt sorry for Alex.
He got out of line and put his
bleach-bottle Santa in Alex's hand.
"Here, you can put it on the tree,"
he said.
Anna Maria said very loudly,
"You're just wasting your nice

Santa Claus on that boy."

But the teacher smiled at Jim.

At the Christmas party,

Alex was the fastest relay runner.

He won for Anna Maria's team.

George said, "Alex can run faster

than any pony!"

After the party, Alex said to Jim,

"I don't really have a pony."

"That's all right," said Jim, "you're the best runner in first grade!"
Anna Maria was listening.
"And that's the truth!" she said.